퇴근

퇴근
Homecoming

천명관 | 전미세리 옮김
Written by Cheon Myeong-kwan
Translated by Jeon Miseli

ASIA
PUBLISHERS

Contents

퇴근
Homecoming

남자는 줄을 놓치지 않기 위해 앞사람 뒤에 바짝 붙어선 채, 아이의 손을 꼭 붙잡고 있었다. 운동장처럼 넓은 고용공단 사무실은 길게 늘어선 수천 명의 실업자들과 어저스터라고 불리는 조정관들, 줄 사이를 날쌔게 오가며 찌라시를 나눠주는 삐끼들이 한데 뒤엉켜 마치 새벽의 암시장처럼 시끄러웠다. 찌라시 중에는 핵공격을 받은 중동에 투입될 용병을 모집하거나 제약회사의 피실험자를 뽑는 안내문도 있었지만 대부분은 장기판매를 권하는 내용이었다. 찌라시엔 다음과 같은 문안이 한글로 적혀 있었다.

A man was waiting in line, holding a child tightly by the hand. He was trying to stay close to the person before *him* so as not to lose his spot. The office of the Employment Corporation, as large as a playing field, was clamorous like the black market early in the morning, packed with thousands of people out of work, standing in long queues, the coordinators, called "adjusters," and the "touts" distributing flyers, nimbly threading their way in and out of the queues. Some flyers were for recruiting mercenaries to be dispatched to the Middle East, which had been attacked with nuclear weapons, others for inviting people to participate in experiments conducted by pharmaceutical companies.

당신의 마지막 자산을 헐값에 넘기시겠습니까?

—휴, 끝이 없구먼. 도대체 이 담요들은 다 얼마나 되
는 거야?

얼굴에 개기름이 번들거리는 한 조정관이 길게 하품
을 하며 투덜거렸다. 담요는 국가운영부에서 지급하는
바우처에 기대 살아가는 사람들을 가리키는 말이었다.
그들은 아무데도 소속되어 있지 않았고 아무 소득이 없
었으며 태반은 일정한 주거지도 없는 노숙자들이었다.
그들을 담요 혹은 블랭킷이라고 부르게 된 것은 추위를
피하기 위해 늘 넝마 같은 담요를 두르고 다니기 때문
이었다.

—글세, 국가운영부에선 삼백만이라지만 실제론 오
백만이 넘는다는 얘기도 있던데……

—젠장, 이렇게 공짜로 퍼주다간 결국 나라를 말아먹
고 말 거야. 이것들을 다 기름을 짜서 비누로 만들어버
릴 수도 없고……

옆자리의 뚱뚱한 조정관이 설탕이 듬뿍 묻은 도넛을
한입 베어물며 말을 받았다.

—그건 아마 비용도 안 나올걸요. 차라리 돼지처럼 한

But most were for trafficking in human organs, with a message printed in Korean such as:

Would you sell off your last remaining property for a song?

"Whew! These lines are endless. How many of them blankets are there, anyways?" a coordinator with a greasy complexion grumbled with a long yawn. "Blankets" meant those who relied on vouchers as their only means of living, issued monthly by the National Administration. They had no affiliation, no income, and, most of them, no home. They were called "blankets" because of the ragged blankets in which they wrapped themselves against the cold.

"Well, the National Administration says there are three million of them now, but I've also heard that it could be over five million—"

"Damn it! If this freeloading continues, it'll bring the country to ruin. You don't suppose we can squeeze grease out of them to make soap, do you?" yet another, fat coordinator sitting next to him chimed in, taking a bite out of a sugar-smothered doughnut.

"That won't even cover the costs. A better way

꺼번에 구덩이에 쓸어넣고 살처분을 하는 게 낫지.

안경을 쓴 젊은 조정관이 자판을 두드리며 으스스하게 웃었다. 주변에 서 있던 담요들은 자신을 조롱하는 끔찍한 농담에도 아무런 반응을 보이지 않고 눈치만 살폈다. 자칫 조정관의 비위를 잘못 건드려 바우처를 못 받게 된다면 앞으로 한 달간은 끔찍한 지옥이 될 게 뻔하기 때문이었다.

─4506번!

머리가 반쯤 벗어진 조정관이 번호를 부르자 남자는 재빨리 그의 앞으로 다가가 서류를 내밀었다. 그것은 그동안 직업을 얻기 위해 어떤 노력을 했는지에 대한 경위와 앞으로 어떤 계획을 가지고 있는지에 대한 보고서였다. 단지 형식적인 절차에 불과하더라도 바우처를 받기 위해선 반드시 필요한 서류로, 사내는 보고서를 작성하느라 꼬박 한나절을 씨름해야 했다.

─아직 나이도 젊고 사지도 멀쩡한데 왜 일을 못 구해?

조정관은 남자에게 눈길도 주지 않고 보고서를 건성으로 들여다보았다. 늘 반복되는 뻔한 얘기였다. 실업률이 구십 퍼센트를 넘어선 지 십 년이 넘어 직업을 구

would be sweeping them all into a pit and burying them like we do with pigs," a young, spectacled coordinator laughed eerily, typing at a keyboard. The blankets standing around them heard the horrible ridicule targeted at them, but showed no response, except for carefully studying the coordinators' faces. They knew that carelessly offending a coordinator could make them lose vouchers, followed by a month of living hell.

"4—5—0—6!"

Called by a half-bald coordinator, the man scrambled to him and held out his document. It was his report explaining how hard he had tried to get a job and what his plans were for future employment. Although nothing but red tape, the report was a must to get a voucher, so he had struggled a whole day to complete it.

"You're still young and able-bodied! Why can't you find work?" the coordinator scanned through the report half-heartedly, not even glancing at the man. The accusation, which had been repeated to him so many times before, failed to inspire the man. The unemployment rate had remained above 90 percent for 10 years, and finding any work had become as wild a dream as going to Heaven after death. But the coordinators had always lashed out

하는 건 이제 죽어서 천국에 간다는 얘기만큼이나 허황한 꿈이 되었다. 그런데도 조정관들은 언제나 모든 책임이 실업자들에게 있다는 듯 호되게 몰아붙이곤 했다.

―아이가 천식이 있어서 약을 먹어야 하거든요. 약값이 너무 비싸서……

남자는 머리를 조아린 채 변명을 하다 슬그머니 말꼬리를 흐렸다. 자칫 불평분자처럼 보일까봐 두려웠기 때문이었다. 한번 불평분자로 낙인이 찍히면 일자리는커녕 알량한 보조금조차 받을 수 없는 처지였다. 하지만 조정관은 그의 말에는 관심이 없는 듯 뒤에 서 있는 아이에게 눈길을 돌렸다. 얼굴을 덮은 하얀 마스크 위로 아이의 겁먹은 눈이 반짝거리고 있었다.

―왜 능력도 없는데 애를 낳아서 고생이야.

조정관의 말에 남자는 울컥 화가 치밀었지만 그의 말이 틀린 것은 아니었다. 회사원도 아닌 주제에 대책도 없이 아이를 낳은 건 분명 그의 잘못이었다. 입을 다물 수밖에 없었다.

―그래서 언제까지 끼고 있을 거야?

―예?

―애 말이야. 학교는 다녀?

at the unemployed, as if they were solely responsible for the situation.

"My child has asthma and needs medicine. And it's so expensive—" the man began making excuses, his head bowed, but soon his voice trailed away in mid-sentence. He was afraid of looking like a complainer. Once branded as such, he would have to forget about the trifle of a voucher, let alone finding any work. The coordinator, though, didn't seem interested in his excuses; instead, he turned his eyes on the child standing behind the man. There was a frightened look in the child's eyes above the white gauze mask that covered most of his face.

"You had the nerve to have a child! You can't even feed it, can you? Well, you asked for it!"

The man felt the surge of anger, but thought the coordinator's remark was not entirely wrong. Obviously it had been his fault to decide to raise a family when he was not an office worker. He had no choice but to keep silent.

"So, until when are you gonna keep him?"

"I beg your pardon?"

"I mean the kid. Is he in school yet?"

"No, not yet—perhaps later, when things are better."

―아, 아직…… 나중에 형편이 나아지면 보내야죠.

조정관의 질책에 남자는 깡마른 몸이 더 쪼그라드는
기분이었다. 조정관은 서류를 내려놓고 은근한 어조로
입을 열었다.

―내가 다니는 교회에 장로님이 한 분 계시거든. 근데
보통 믿음이 아니셔. 헌금도 많이 내고. 부인도 몇 번 봤
지만 두 분 다 인상이 그렇게 좋을 수가 없더라고.

남자는 조정관이 하려는 말이 무엇인지 금세 알아차
렸다.

―게다가 어찌나 애들을 좋아하는지 불쌍한 애들만
보면 튀기고 뭐고 가리지 않고 다 거둬주셔. 정말 사랑
이 넘치는 분들이지.

비록 아이가 커다란 마스크로 얼굴을 가리고 있어도 조
정관은 그가 혼혈이라는 것을 금세 알아챈 모양이었다.

아이의 엄마는 깊고 커다란 눈과 카페오레처럼 아름
다운 피부색을 가진 인도 여자였다. 그녀는 남편의 학
대를 피해 뱅골 만을 건넌 뒤 미얀마와 태국을 거쳐 한
국까지 흘러들어왔는데, 두 사람이 만난 건 한 가죽공
장의 작업장에서였다. 살이 녹아나는 지독한 화학약품
의 독성과 썩어가는 가죽의 악취 속에서도 두 사람은

At the coordinator's reproachful question, the man felt his thin body shriveling further. The coordinator put down the document and began telling him in a secretive tone.

"One of the elders in my church—now, there's a man of devotion for you. He also makes generous contributions to the church. I've seen his wife a few times, too. The couple has made such a great impression on me."

The man immediately understood what the coordinator was trying to say.

"Moreover, they love children so much that they've taken so many unfortunate kids under their wing, whether they're mixed blood or not. They have so much love to give."

Although the child's face was hidden under the big mask, the coordinator seemed to have noticed him being half-blooded right away.

The child's mother had been Indian, with big, serene eyes and skin color as beautiful as café au lait. She had crossed the Bay of Bengal to escape from her abusive husband, passed through Myanmar and Thailand, wandered onto the Korean Peninsula, and met the man while both of them were working at a hide tanning factory. Even exposed to the danger of flesh-melting, toxic chemicals and the stench of

첫눈에 사랑에 빠졌고 곧 동거를 시작했다. 하지만 힘겹게 시작한 사랑은 채 몇 년도 지나지 않아 위기를 맞았다. 아이를 낳은 지 이 년 만에 공장이 아프리카로 옮겨가며 일자리를 잃고 만 것이다. 비록 쥐꼬리만 한 임금이었어도 일자리가 있을 땐 어떻게든 버틸 수 있었지만 공장이 문을 닫고 나자 더는 생계를 이어갈 방도가 없었다. 결국 이듬해 겨울, 여자는 서툰 한글로 쓴 짧은 편지를 한 장 남기고 사라졌다.

정말 미안해요. 나도 어쩔 수 업서요. 부듸 용서해주세요. 당신을 사랑하는 프리야.

그 후, 남자는 여자가 암시장 근처에서 몸을 팔며 살아간다는 소문과 중국으로 떠났다는 소문을 번갈아가며 들었다.

─그래서 말인데……

조정관은 큼, 목을 가다듬고 드디어 본론을 꺼냈다.

─내가 그분들한테 애를 입양할 수 있게 잘 얘기해줄 수 있거든.

조정관은 먹잇감을 발견한 맹수처럼 입맛을 다셨다. 남자는 힐끗 뒤를 돌아보다 아이와 눈이 마주쳤다. 오도카니 서 있는 아이의 눈은 엄마를 닮아 크고 슬퍼 보

rotting hide, the two had fallen in love and soon began living together. But their hard-earned love lasted only a few years before they faced a crisis. Two years after they had a child, the factory moved to Africa and they lost their jobs. Although their wages hadn't been much, they had somehow managed to eke out a living. Once the factory was gone, however, they had no other means for making a living. The next winter, his wife disappeared, leaving behind a short letter, written in broken Korean:

"I'm really sory. I don now wat else to do. Pleaz, forgive me. I love you. Friya"

A while later, he heard some people saying that she was walking the streets near the black market and others that she had gone to China.

"What I mean to say is—"

The coordinator cleared his throat and got down to his main point.

"I can talk the couple into adopting your kid, if you want me to."

The coordinator smacked his lips like a savage beast that had just spotted a prey. The man glanced back and caught the eyes of his child standing alone behind him. His eyes looked just like his mother's, big and sad.

였다.

—자네 입장만 생각하지 말고 아이의 장래를 생각해 보라고. 낳기만 한다고 다 자식이 아냐. 밥 한 끼도 제대로 못 먹이는데 그걸 부모라고 할 수 있겠어?

조정관이 굳이 입양을 주선하겠다고 나서는 건 보나마나 거액의 사례비 때문이었다.

몇 년 전부터 슈퍼리치들 사이에선 아이를 입양하는 게 유행이었다. 그것은 자신의 능력을 과시하는 한편 노블레스 오블리주를 실천할 수 있는 수단으로 작용해, 슈퍼리치들은 경쟁적으로 더 많은 입양아를 원했고, 한 가정의 입양아들로만 구성된 축구단이나 성가대를 심심찮게 볼 수 있었다. 최근 팔순을 맞은 한 슈퍼리치는 자신의 나이에 맞춰 여든 명의 아이들을 한꺼번에 입양해 화제가 되기도 했는데, 아이들은 그의 생일파티에서 유니폼을 맞춰입고 부자 아버지를 맞은 행운을 뮤지컬로 표현한 축하공연을 선보였다고 했다.

입양 대상은 당연히 담요에서 나서 담요에서 자란 담요의 아이들이었다. 그것은 변덕스러운 슈퍼리치들이 한때 열을 올렸던 희귀 나비 수집이나 우주 관광, 또는 누드 라이딩처럼 잠시의 유행으로 끝날 게 뻔했지만 조

"You should stop being selfish and think of the kid's future. Giving birth isn't enough. Can you call yourself a parent when you can't even feed your child?"

There was no doubt that the coordinator was volunteering to arrange the adoption because of the large reward that would fall in his way, once it was carried through.

For a few years, it had been a trend among the super-rich to adopt children. Taking it as an opportunity to show off their power as well as to practice noblesse oblige, the super-rich had competitively adopted child after child. Consequently, it was not uncommon to see a soccer team or a choir composed of children who had been adopted into one and the same family. One rich man had become the talk of the town by adopting 80 children on the occasion of his 80th birthday. It was said that during the old man's birthday party, all of the children, dressed in uniform, had performed a musical composed to celebrate their good luck in having the rich man as their foster father.

Needless to say, all of the adoptees were blanket children, born of and raised by blankets. Apparently, it was another whim of the super-rich, like collecting rare butterflies, space travel, or nude

정관들에겐 몸뚱이만 남은 담요들 틈에서 짭짤한 수입을 올릴 좋은 기회이기도 했다.

—제가 아직 입양은 생각을 못 해봤거든요. 그래서 지금은 당장 뭐라고 드릴 말씀이 없네요.

남자는 조정관의 호의를 무시한다는 뉘앙스를 주지 않기 위해 최대한 공손하게, 하지만 의지는 분명하게 대답했다. 그러자 조정관은 쩝쩝, 입맛을 다시며 전화번호가 적혀 있는 명함을 한 장 내밀었다.

—하나님도 영접할 준비가 돼 있는 자에게만 은혜를 베푸는 법이야. 기회가 있을 때 빨리 결정하라고.

그러고는 서류에 꽝, 소리가 나게 도장을 찍었다.

*

—아빠 왜 안 먹어?

아이가 정신없이 햄버거를 먹다 문득 생각난 듯 남자를 올려다보았다.

—응, 아빠 아까 많이 먹었어.

—언제?

—아까 너 잘 때.

horseback riding, which had been the rage one moment and become passé the next. Nonetheless, it was a chance for the coordinators to raise a sizable amount of extra income by taking advantage of the blankets, who had nothing left but their children's bodies to offer.

"I haven't thought about adoption yet... so, I can't tell you anything at the moment."

While making his intention clear, the man did his utmost to appear respectful to the coordinator, who might have taken his answer as an offense against his goodwill. The coordinator smacked his lips again and held out to the man a calling card with a phone number printed on it.

"Even God blesses those who are ready to accept His grace. Grab this chance quickly before it flies away."

Then he brought down a seal on the man's document with a loud thud.

*

"Daddy, why aren't you eating?" the boy suddenly raised his head from the hamburger he had been gulping down.

"Don't worry. I've already had plenty."

이때, 남자의 배에서 꼬르륵 소리가 났다. 그는 민망한 소리를 숨기기 위해 짐짓 너털웃음을 터트렸다. 그리고 아이의 입에 묻은 소스를 가리키며 말했다.

—너 입에 묻은 거 보니까 꼭 원숭이 같아.

—원숭이? 이, 씨! 나 원숭이 아냐.

아이는 아빠를 때리는 시늉을 하고 다시 햄버거에 얼굴을 박았다. 햄버거는 빵과 채소, 고기패티가 짙은 갈색의 소스와 함께 질척하게 버무려져 흡사 쓰레기통에 버려진 라자냐 덩어리처럼 보였다. 그래도 아이가 한 끼 배불리 먹을 수 있어 다행이었다. 남자 또한 하루종일 굶어 허리가 꺾일 것 같았지만 귀한 바우처를 함부로 낭비할 순 없었다. 바우처는 따로 쓸데가 있었다. 그래서 기회가 있을 때마다 수돗물을 양껏 들이켜 배를 채웠다.

담요들이 이용하는 전용식당 안은 그날 바우처를 지급받은 사람들로 가득 차 싸구려 음식들로 다들 허겁지겁 배를 채우고 있었지만 아무런 활기도 웃음소리도 없었다. 단지 시큼한 음식 냄새와 무거운 공기가 그들의 어깨를 짓누르고 있었다. 공단 사무실에서 만났던 지인들도 몇 명 눈에 띄었지만 남자는 애써 고개를 돌려 외

"When?"

"Just now, while you were sleeping."

At the moment, the man's stomach growled. He burst out laughing to cover the embarrassing noise. Pointing at the sauce smeared around the child's mouth, he said: "You look like a chimp with that sauce around your mouth."

"A chimp? No, Daddy! I'm not a chimp."

The kid made a feint of punching his father, before burying his face in the hamburger again. The hamburger looked like a lump of lasagna dumped in the garbage can, with the bun, vegetables, and meat patty mixed up in a gooey, dark brown sauce. Nevertheless, he felt happy to see his child eating his fill, if only for just that once. The man himself had had nothing to eat the whole day. He was on the verge of doubling up with hunger. But he was determined not to waste his vouchers carelessly; he needed them for another purpose. So he kept filling his stomach with tap water whenever he had a chance.

The diner designated for the blankets was packed with those who had received vouchers that day. Although people were hastily stuffing their stomachs with the cheap food, the inside of the diner was devoid of liveliness or laughter. Only the

면했다.

실업자의 숫자가 한계치를 넘어서자 거리 곳곳에서 시위와 폭동이 일어났다. 남자도 몇 번 폭동에 가담한 적이 있었다. 계엄령이 선포되고 경찰과 군인에 의해 많은 사람이 목숨을 잃었다. 폭동이 진압된 후, 국가운영부는 고용공단을 통해 실업자들에게 바우처를 나눠주기 시작했다. 그것은 전용식당을 이용하거나 공단이 운영하는 마켓에서 생필품을 구할 수 있는 쿠폰의 일종이었다. 하지만 지급된 바우처로는 입에 풀칠하는 것조차 힘겨워 결국 아무것도 변한 게 없었다. 아니, 오히려 상황은 더 악화되었다. 바우처가 시장에 풀리면서 인플레이션을 부추긴 것이다. 가뜩이나 높았던 물가가 한 계단 더 뛰어오르자 우수수, 낙엽이 떨어지듯 다시 수많은 실업자가 담요를 두른 채 거리로 내몰렸다.

—아빠.

햄버거를 다 먹고 남은 탄산음료를 빨아먹던 아이가 남자에게 말했다.

—응, 왜?

—난 이다음에 커서 회사원이 될 거야.

—회사원?

sour smell of food and a sense of heaviness pressed down on their shoulders. The man recognized a few acquaintances he had met in the office of the Employment Corporation, but he looked away deliberately.

As the number of unemployed had increased beyond a tolerable limit, demonstrations and riots had begun to take place in the streets. The man had joined several riots. Martial law had been proclaimed and many people had been killed by the police and army. After the riots had been put down, the National Administration had begun issuing vouchers to the unemployed through the Employment Corporation. The vouchers could be used like coupons for eating at designated diners or buying daily necessities at the markets run by the Corporation. But with the vouchers alone, one could hardly feed oneself, which meant nothing had changed. Rather, things had gotten worse, since the vouchers circulating in the markets had caused inflation. The already-high prices jumped further, and as autumn leaves fall in great masses in a gust of wind, countless people had lost their jobs and were driven out of their homes onto the street, wrapped in a blanket as their only possession.

Having finished the hamburger and noisily

남자는 놀라 쳐다보았다.

—회사원이 뭐하는 사람인지는 알아?

—알아, 회사에 다니는 사람이잖아.

—그럼 회사가 뭔데?

아이한텐 너무 어려운 질문이었을까? 아이는 잠시 골똘히 생각하다 손가락으로 창밖을 가리켰다.

—저기…… 저거.

아이가 가리키는 손끝 멀리, 강 건너엔 거대한 빌딩 숲이 서 있었다. 그곳은 금융회사들이 밀집해 있는 증권가로, 담요들은 함부로 출입할 수 없는 구역이었다.

슈퍼리치들은 더 이상 상품을 만들지 않았다. 대신 돈을 굴려 돈을 버는 자본소득에만 열을 올렸다. 공장도 기계도, 골치 아픈 노동자도 까다로운 소비자도 필요 없었다. 돈을 굴리는 일은 소수의 전문가만 있으면 가능한 일이어서 고용도 문제가 아니었다. 자본은 국경을 자유롭게 넘나들며 아메바처럼 스스로 증식을 거듭해 괴물처럼 점점 더 몸집을 불려나갔다. 반면에 한때는 성실한 노동자였고 순진한 소비자였던 이들은 이제 짜봐야 똥밖에 안 나오는 쓸모없는 담요로 전락하고 말았다.

—근데 그런 말은 누구한테 들었어?

sucked the straw to drink up the remaining soda pop, the boy called his father:

"Daddy!"

"Yes?"

"I'll become an office worker when I grow up."

"An office worker?" the man stared at the boy in surprise. "Do you even know what an office worker is?"

"I know. It's a man who works in a company office."

"What then is a company?"

Perhaps it was too difficult a question for a child to answer. Mulling over it for a while, the boy pointed his finger at something outside the window.

"There—that one over there," he was pointing at the massive forest of buildings far away on the other side of the river. It was the stock market, densely populated with financial firms, and off-limits to the blanket.

The super-rich no longer made products. Instead, they were focused on generating capital income—money gotten by manipulating other money. There were no more factories, machinery, troublesome laborers, or difficult consumers. Human resources management was not a problem

―토끼 아줌마한테.

토끼는 남자가 볼일이 있을 때마다 아이를 맡기곤 하
는 이웃집 독신녀였다. 그녀는 아이의 엄마, 프리야의
친구이기도 했는데 불행하게도 선천적인 알비노증후
군이어서 토끼처럼 빨간 눈에 백설처럼 하얀 머리카락
과 피부색을 가지고 있었다. 그 때문인지 그녀는 외출
도 안 하고 늘 술에 취해 컴컴한 골방에만 틀어박혀 있
었다.

―회사에 가면 큰 책상이 있대. 근데 그게 자기 혼자
쓰는 책상이래.

아이는 눈을 반짝이며 계속 떠들었다.

―그리고 사무실이 아주 높은 데 있어서 비행기가 옆
으로 지나가는 것도 볼 수 있대. 비행기에 타고 있는 사
람한테 손도 흔들고. 그리고 또…… 아, 맞다! 커피하고
도넛도 마음대로 먹을 수 있대!

아이의 얘기를 들으며 남자는 피식 웃었다. 언제나 토
끼굴처럼 어두컴컴한 오피스텔에 처박혀서 술만 먹는
주정뱅이가 회사가 어떻게 생겼는지 알 리 없었다. 아
마도 어디서 주워들은 얘기를 한껏 과장해 아이에게 떠
벌린 모양이었다. 그런데 이때, 남자는 문득 어릴 때 그

anymore, since manipulating money required only a few experts. Capital freely crossed the borders and self-proliferated like amoebas into monstrous sizes. Meanwhile, formerly hard-working laborers and naive consumers turned into blankets who would produce nothing but shit when squeezed.

"By the way, who told you all that?"

"Aunt Rabbit."

Aunt Rabbit was his neighbor, a single woman whom he asked to look after his child whenever he had something to do outside. She had also been a friend of Friya's. Unfortunately, the woman was born an albino, with red eyes, snow-white hair, and skin like a rabbit. That was most likely the reason she never left home, shutting herself up in a dark backroom, and always drunk.

"Aunt Rabbit says there's a big desk in the company office. And you can use it all by yourself."

The child prattled on, its eyes twinkling.

"And the office is so high up there and you can even see an airplane flying by you and wave to the people in it. And—yeah! you can eat all the coffee and doughnuts you want!"

Listening to the child, the man smiled listlessly. It was impossible for his drunkard neighbor, always cooped up in her office-hotel as dark as the rabbit's

의 아버지와 나누었던 대화의 한 장면이 떠올랐다.

언제인지 정확히 기억도 나지 않을 만큼 오래전의 일이었다. 그의 아버지가 밥을 먹다 말고 장래희망이 뭐냐고 물었을 때, 당시 아이 또래였던 남자는 변신로봇이 되고 싶다고 했다.

―변신로봇?

아버지가 눈을 크게 뜨고 되물었다. 변신로봇은 당시 영화를 통해 유행하던 캐릭터였다. 평소엔 자동차였다가 위험한 상황이 되면 로봇으로 변신해서 싸우는 트랜스포머는 남자아이들이 가장 선망하는 영웅이었다. 당시 유행어로 그들이 '짱' 좋아하는 로봇과 자동차를 한몸에 구현한 캐릭터였으니 당연히 그럴 법도 했다.

실제로 그의 평생의 꿈은 변신과 합체였다. 절대 부서지지 않는 금속성의 육체와 모든 것을 파괴할 수 있는 무한한 파워. 그래서 가난도 고통도 모르는 불멸의 히어로…… 하지만 그는 변신에도, 그리고 합체에도 실패해 직업도, 아내도 없이 혼자 아이를 키우는 고달픈 담요 신세가 되고 말았다.

그렇게 이룰 수 없는 꿈은 대를 물려 이어지는 것인가? 아이가 회사원이 되는 건 변신로봇이 되는 것만큼

burrow, to know what a company office looked like. Perhaps she exaggerated what she had picked up elsewhere. At the moment, the man had a flashback to a conversation he had had as a child with his father.

It had been so long that he didn't remember exactly when. During a meal, his father had asked him what he wanted to be when he grew up. Perhaps around his boy's age at the time, he had answered that he wanted to be a Transformer.

"A Transformer?" his father opened his eyes wide. Transformer had been a popular movie character at the time. The character usually stayed in the shape of a car, but in a crisis, it would transform itself into a fighter robot. It was the most admired hero among the boys of the time, which was natural since Transformer was a robot and a car, two of their "ultra-favorite"—to use the fad expression in those days—things united into one.

In fact, his lifelong dream had been for transformation and union. An unbreakable metallic body with unlimited power that can destroy everything. An immortal hero free from hunger or pain. But, he had failed at both transformation and union, ending up jobless and wifeless, a weary blanket raising a child single-handedly.

이나 불가능한 일이었다. 그래서 오래전 그의 아버지가 그랬듯이 그는 아이를 보며 허허, 웃기만 했다.

기실, 그의 아버지는 회사원이었다. 비록 오래전 일이지만 당시엔 회사원이 그리 특별한 직업이 아니었다. 아버지의 친구들도 모두 회사원이었고 친구들의 아버지도 회사원이었다. 그들은 언제나 넥타이를 매고 있었는데 그가 기억하는 회사원이란 구겨진 양복과 찌든 얼굴, 구두약을 바른 듯 거뭇해진 수염을 턱에 매단 채 밤늦게 술냄새를 풍기며 들어오던 초췌한 중년의 사내들이었다. 하지만 실업률이 구십 퍼센트를 넘어서자 회사원은 이전과 다른 특별한 신분이 되었다.

한편, 실업률이 늘어나고 경기침체가 길게 이어지자 회사에 적을 두지 못한 사람들은 빠르게 몰락해갔다. 중산층에서 빈민층으로 빈민층에서 담요로 떨어지기까지 채 십 년도 걸리지 않았다. 상대적으로 회사원의 신분은 점점 더 높이 올라가 급기야 그들이 이용하는 식당이 따로 생겨났고 화장실도 일반인용과 회사원용이 분리되었다. 강 건너 남쪽에 위치한 백화점이나 고급 음식점은 회사 배지가 없으면 아예 출입이 불가능했다. 인종이 아닌 계급에 의해 생겨난 신종 아파르트헤

Is an unachievable dream passed down from one generation to the next? His child's becoming an office worker seemed as impossible as his changing into a transformer robot. Now, all he could do was look at his child and give a helpless laugh, as his father had done a long time before.

In fact, his father, who was now only a childhood memory, had been an office worker. Back then, having a white-collar job at a company had not been so special. Friends of his father's had all been office workers and so had all of his own friends' fathers. He remembered the office workers of the olden days as shabby-looking, middle-aged men always wearing a necktie, a wrinkled-up suit, and a dark afternoon shadow, as if they had shoe polish on their haggard faces. Once the unemployment rate increased to more than 90 percent, however, office workers had become a class with high status.

As the unemployment rate rose even further and economic recession was prolonged, people who were not on any payroll quickly fell to ruin. It took less than 10 years to fall from the middle class to the poor and needy, and then to a blanket. Meanwhile, the status of office workers kept rising, until there sprang up restaurants and even washrooms reserved for them. The department stores and

이트였다. 처음엔 물론 반발이 있었지만 언제나 그렇듯이 사람들은 곧 새로운 시스템에 익숙해졌다.

그런데 왜 아버지는 우리를 버렸을까?

남은 빵 부스러기를 핥아먹는 아이를 바라보는 동안 남자의 머릿속에선 오랜 의문이 되살아났다. 아버지가 사라진 건 그가 열 살이 되던 해였다. 엄마와 여동생, 그리고 자신을 버리고 집을 나가버린 거였다. 변명도 사과도, 그리고 작별인사도 없었다. 엄마는 아버지에게 다른 여자가 생긴 거라고 했다. 하지만 당시의 그는 엄마의 말이 무슨 뜻인지 이해하지 못했다. 이후, 남은 가족은 말할 수 없이 혹독한 시절을 보내야 했다.

―다 먹었으면 그만 나가자.

남자는 고통스런 기억을 떨쳐내듯 자리에서 벌떡 일어났다. 그리고 빈 빨대를 쪽쪽 소리나게 빨고 있는 아이의 손을 잡고 식당을 나섰다. 토끼가 술에 취해 정신줄을 놓기 전에 아이를 맡기려면 서둘러야 했다.

*

새벽의 암시장은 언제나 눈이 매울 만큼 매캐한 연기

high-class restaurants located south of the river were not accessible to those without a company badge. It was a new version of apartheid created not by racial but class discrimination. Of course, there had been resistance at the beginning; but people soon learned to adjust themselves to the new system.

But then, why did my father desert us? While watching his child licking up the bread crumbs, the old question revived in his mind. His father had walked out on his family—his mother, his younger sister, and him—when he was 10. His father had made no excuse, apology, or farewell. His mother told him that his father had met another woman, but he didn't understand what that meant. From that time on, his family had endured hardships beyond description.

"If you're done, let's go."

The man jumped to his feet, as if shaking off the painful memory. Hand in hand with his child, still sucking loudly on the empty straw, they left the diner. The man had to hurry if he wanted to leave his child in Aunt Rabbit's care before she got too drunk and lost her senses.

*

가 가득 차 있었다. 언 몸을 녹이기 위해 사람들이 곳곳에 피워 놓은 화톳불 때문이었다. 커다란 드럼통에 생선상자든 폐타이어든 사리지 않고 던져넣고 늘 시커먼 연기가 시장 하늘을 뒤덮고 있었다.

　—말보로 있어요, 말보로.

　시장 입구에서 한 사내가 남자에게 빠르게 다가와 속삭였다. 순간, 담배를 피우고 싶은 욕망에 목울대가 꿀렁거렸다. 담배를 끊은 지 이십 년이 지났어도 니코틴에 대한 집착은 사라지지 않고 끈질기게 달라붙어 있었다. 국가운영부에서 담배의 제조와 판매를 금지한 금연법 시행 이후, 담배는 암시장에서 가장 인기 있는 품목이 되었다. 그다음으로 인기가 좋은 건 술이었고 그다음이 환각제였다. 비록 나락으로 떨어진 담요들이었지만 쾌락을 좇는 열정만은 정상인과 하등 다를 바 없었다.

　남자는 담배장수의 손길을 뿌리치고 시장 안으로 들어섰다. 바우처를 지급받은 날이면 시장 골목마다 수많은 담요들이 시궁창의 쥐떼처럼 들끓었다. 원래 바우처는 지정식당이나 전용마켓에서만 쓸 수 있도록 법으로 정해져 있었다. 하지만 그것은 곧 암시장에서 화폐처럼 통용되었고 술이나 담배, 마약 등을 조달하는 데 이용

Early in the morning, the black market, as always, was filled with thick, eye-smarting smoke from the bonfires made here and there by the dealers to warm themselves. They tossed everything—fish crates, waste tires, and other detritus—into the fire in big drum cans, so that clouds of black smoke always hung low over the market.

"I've got Marlboro. Marlboro!" At the entrance to the market, a seller nimbly approached and whispered to him. Suddenly, he was overwhelmed by such a strong desire to smoke that he felt his Adam's apple squirm. He had quit smoking 20 years before, and yet his craving for nicotine had persisted. After the National Administration outlawed the manufacture and sale of cigarettes, they became the most popular item in the black markets. Second was liquor, followed by psychedelic drugs. Although struggling in abysmal ruins, "blankets" were as zealous as any other people when it came to pursuing pleasure.

The man shook off the cigarette dealer's hand and entered the market. On the voucher days, all alleys in the black markets teemed with blankets, as in the rat-infested sewer. According to the law, vouchers were supposed to be used only in the designated diners or markets; but they quickly be-

되었다. 그렇게 암시장은 담요들의 바우처를 기반으로 도시경제의 한 축을 담당할 만큼 크게 성장했다.

시장 중간쯤엔 창녀들이 길을 막고 있었다. 가진 거라 곤 몸뚱이 하나밖에 없는 중년의 담요부대들이었다.

—미스터, 이리 좀 와봐. 오늘 해피하게 해줄게.

농구공처럼 얼굴이 크고 동그란 여자가 공처럼 스르 르 굴러와 남자의 팔짱을 꼈다. 농구공만한 젖가슴이 뭉클, 팔꿈치를 짓눌렀다.

—바우처 한 장만 내면 입으로 해줄게. 인터코스는 두 장, 세 장이면 애널도 가능한데, 어때? 오늘 개시도 못 해서 아직 버진이거든.

여자의 뜨거운 입김이 귀를 간지럽혔다. 순간, 남자는 아랫도리가 뜨거워졌다. 하지만 순간의 유혹에 넘어가 바우처를 써버렸다간 한 달 내내 어떤 고생을 할지 눈 에 훤했다. 자리를 막 뜨려는데 골목 끝에 서 있는 한 여 자가 눈에 들어왔다. 허리가 잘록하고 카페오레처럼 짙 은 갈색의 피부를 가진 여자였다. 그녀는 짧은 치마를 입고 가로등 아래에 서서 지나가는 손님들을 향해 손을 흔들고 있었다.

—프리야?

gan circulating like legal currency in black markets, especially those supplying liquor, cigarettes, and drugs. Thus, with the blanket's vouchers, black markets had grown into one of the financial mainstays of the city.

About the center of the market, a group of prostitutes blocked the way: middle-aged blankets whose only possession was their body.

"Hey Mister, come over here. I'll make you happy today."

A woman with a big, round face like a basketball came up to him, as spontaneously as a rolling ball, and linked arms with him. Her soft breast, also as large as a basketball, pressed against his elbow.

"One voucher for oral, two for intercourse, with three even anal's possible. What d'you say? Haven't made a first sale yet, so I'm still a virgin today."

The woman's warm breath tickled his ear. Instantly, he felt hot below the waist. Nevertheless, he knew well what kinds of hardship he would face the whole following month if he gave in to the temptation and spent the voucher there. When he was about to leave her, he happened to catch sight of another woman standing at the end of the alley. She had a slender waist and dark brown skin, like café au lait. In a short skirt, she was waving to the

남자는 창녀의 손을 뿌리치고 여자를 향해 허겁지겁 달려갔다.

─어서 와, 달링.

카페오레 여자가 환하게 웃으며 남자를 반겼다. 하지만 가로등 불빛 아래 드러난 얼굴은 프리야가 아니었다. 흔하디흔한 동남아 혼혈이었다. 잔뜩 실망한 그는 허탈하게 터덜터덜 골목을 빠져나왔다. 뒤에서 '재수없는 새끼!' 어쩌고 하는 여자의 욕설이 들렸다.

─무슨 약값이 그렇게 많이 올라요?

남자가 볼멘소리로 항의를 해봤지만 콧수염을 기른 약장수는 주섬주섬 약가방을 뒤지며 시큰둥하게 대답했다.

─요즘 공급이 달려서 웃돈을 줘도 구하기가 어려워. 그나마 나니까 있는 거지, 다른 데 가면 스테로이드는 구경도 못 해.

남자는 목이 메었다. 배를 곯아가며 겨우 바우처를 모아왔는데 약값이 두 배로 오르다니! 다리에 힘이 풀렸다. 의료보험이 없는 담요들은 아파도 병원에 갈 수 없었다. 아무리 발버둥쳐도 살인적인 의료비를 감당할 수 없기 때문이었다. 그래서 남자는 궁여지책으로 암시장

passers-by.

"Friya?"

The man shook off the prostitute's hand and rushed to the dark-skinned woman.

"Welcome, darling." the café-au-lait woman gave him a broad smile.

But the face revealed by the light of a street lamp was not Friya's. She was just one of the common Southeast Asian half-breeds. Dejected, he trudged out of the alley, the woman cursing from behind him, "Damn bastard!"

"How on earth has the price gone up so much?" the man protested in a sulky tone.

But the mustached drug dealer answered in an ill humor, while rummaging through his merchandise bag, "These days, supplies are short and hard to come by even if one pays extra. You're lucky to have me. You'll find no steroids whatever anywhere else."

The man felt choked up. He had been starving himself in order to save the vouchers, but the price of the medicine had doubled! His legs felt weak. Blankets, who had no medical insurance, couldn't go to a hospital when they fell sick. No matter how hard they struggled, they could not afford to pay

에서 스테로이드를 구해 아이에게 먹였다. 그것이 천식에 얼마나 효과가 있는지, 어떤 부작용이 있는지도 알 수 없지만 아이를 위해 그가 할 수 있는 건 그것뿐이었다.

씨발!

당장 폭발할 듯 분노가 솟구쳤지만 남자는 누구에게 욕을 해야 할지 알 수 없었다. 과거의 어른들은 무슨 일이 됐든 일단 정부를 욕하고 보는 게 보통이었다. 하지만 이미 오래전에 정부는 사라지고 없었다. 욕을 할 대상도 없어졌다. 모든 부와 권력, 정보와 조직을 장악한 슈퍼리치들 밑에서 떡고물을 받아먹으며 충복 노릇을 하던 정부와 관료들은 회사에 흡수되었고 정부의 모든 업무는 채 백 명도 안 되는 회사의 작은 부서로 이관되었다. 그것이 바로 국가운영부였다.

─근데 스테로이드가 씨가 마른 이유가 뭔지 알아?

약장수의 질문에 남자는 먹먹한 얼굴로 쳐다보았다.

─요즘 슈퍼리치 놈들 몇몇이 장난을 치는 모양이야.

─무슨 장난요?

─자기들끼리 담요들 목숨의 가격은 과연 얼마나 될까, 하는 내기를 걸었다나봐.

─그게 스테로이드랑 무슨 상관이에요?

the murderous medical service fees. As a desperate measure to help his sick child, the man had been buying steroids on the black market. He didn't know how effective it was for asthma or if there were any side-effects, but it was all he could do for his child.

"Goddamn!"

He was about to explode with anger, but he didn't know where to direct it. Adults used to blame the government first for everything. But now the government had long gone, and so had its role as the target of people's criticism. The super-rich had taken control of all the wealth, power, information, and systems. The government and its officials, who had been at the super-rich's service while enjoying the bread crumbs falling off their table, were absorbed into the existing companies. All government affairs had been transferred to a small division of a company that had less than 100 employees: the National Administration.

"By the way, do you know why steroids have become scarce?"

The man could only look at the dealer heavy-heartedly.

"It seems that some of the super-rich are playing tricks these days."

―잘 들어봐.

약장수는 얼굴을 바짝 내밀며 말을 이었다.

―스테로이드를 먹는 사람들은 자네 아들처럼 천식
이나 간경화, 폐병처럼 위험한 병을 가진 사람들이야.
그래서 약을 못 먹으면 결국 죽게 돼 있어. 그런데 지금
처럼 약값이 점점 더 오른다면 어떻게 될까? 그랬을 때
과연 담요들은 얼마나 많은 돈을 지불할 수 있을까? 하
는 게 바로 그놈들이 궁금해하는 점이야.

―그래서요?

―그래서 암시장에 풀린 스테로이드의 공급을 조절
하면서 조금씩 가격을 올리고 있는 거지. 더 이상 담요
들이 구입할 수 없을 때까지. 그렇게 한계치를 측정해
담요의 목숨값을 산출한다는 거야.

―도, 도대체 그런 쓸데없는 내기를 왜 하는 거죠?

―그거야 뭐 그냥 재미로 그러는 거 아니겠어?

남자는 분노로 말을 맺지 못했다. 그러자 약장수가 피
식 웃으며 말했다.

―사람 목숨이 아니라 담요 목숨이니까. 자넨 아직 슈
퍼리치가 어떤 놈들인지 모르는구먼. 그놈들은 재미만
있다면 개똥도 주워먹을 놈들이야. 거 왜 못 봤어? 단체

"What tricks?"

"There seems to be a bet laid among them on guessing how much a blanket's life is worth."

"What's that got to do with steroids?"

"Listen to me carefully."

The dealer leaned his face closer to the man's and went on:

"Steroids are used by those with dangerous diseases, like asthma, liver cirrhosis, or tuberculosis, you know, just like your son. That means they'll die if they stop taking them. What d'you think will happen if they keep marking up the price, as they do now? How much is the top limit that blankets are willing to pay for it? That's what the super-rich are trying to figure out."

"So?"

"So, they're raising the price little by little by manipulating the supplies of steroids accordingly in the black market. Until blankets can no longer afford it. That's how they figure on calculating the value of a blanket's life, by estimating the ceiling."

"What—what good is that?"

"Well, just for fun, that's all. What else?"

The man got so angry that his tongue failed him. The dealer added with a scoff, "As for them, it's not human life but the blanket's they're playing with.

로 발가벗고 말 타는 거.

약장수는 퉤, 가래를 내뱉으며 욕을 퍼부었다.

—에이, 재수 없는 새끼들!

*

아이의 목숨의 가치는 얼마나 되는 걸까? 아이의 약
값을 구하기 위해 과연 얼마나 더 비싼 희생을 치를 수
있을까? 암시장에서 약을 구해 나오는 길에 남자의 머
릿속에선 수많은 생각이 떠올랐다. 그에겐 어떤 희생을
치르더라도 아이를 포기할 수 없다는 불꽃같은 의지가
있었다. 그러나 한 끼도 먹지 않고 바우처를 모아도 스
테로이드 한 알조차 살 수 없다면? 남자는 지독한 절망
감에 바닥에 주저앉고 싶은 심정이었다. 하지만 아이가
이틀째 약을 못 먹었다는 생각에 절로 걸음이 바빠졌다.

끼익!

녹슨 철문이 열리는 소리에 오피스텔의 정적이 깨졌
다. 지은 지 백 년이 넘은 오피스텔은 이미 용도폐기되
어 등기상으로는 존재하지 않는 버려진 건물이었다. 그
래서 언제 무너질지 모르는 위험을 안고 있었지만 천장

You still don't know what kind of bastards the super-rich are, do you? They won't hesitate to eat dog shit as long as they have fun doing it. Haven't you seen them? Parties of them riding horses naked."

The dealer cursed, "Goddamn bastards!" hawking up and spitting.

*

How much is my boy's life worth? How much more sacrifice would I be able to make to get the medicine for my child? he wondered. As he left the black market with the medicine, so many thoughts entered his mind. He was of course determined not to give up on his child at any cost. But what if he saved as many vouchers as he could by skipping meal after meal, and yet couldn't buy even a tablet of steroid? A sense of profound despair made him feel like dropping to his knees. Nevertheless, he couldn't help forcing himself to quicken his pace, remembering that his son had gone without the medicine for two whole days.

The rusty iron door squeaked open and broke the silence inside the office-hotel suite. The 100-year-old office-hotel had been abandoned

이 있어 비를 막아주기만 한다면 담요들은 감지덕지였다. 실제로 버려진 아파트나 오피스텔이 하루아침에 폭삭 주저앉아 수백 명의 담요들이 한꺼번에 목숨을 잃는 일이 드물지 않았는데도 건물에 깔려 죽는 것을 두려워하는 담요는 아무도 없었다.

오래전, 회사원들이 강 건너 남쪽으로 이주해 자리를 잡자 폐허가 된 시내의 북쪽 건물들은 모두 담요들 차지가 되었다. 대부분 불법점거였지만 경찰도 굳이 나서서 쫓아내려고 하지 않았기 때문에 공동화가 된 시내는 희생자를 찾아 하이에나처럼 어슬렁거리는 청년단 패거리들 이외엔 아무도 들어가고 싶어하지 않는 거대한 슬럼가가 되어버렸다.

문을 열고 안으로 들어섰을 때 어둠 속에서 술냄새가 날아와 코를 찔렀다. 그리고 동시에 아이의 신음이 들렸다. 꺼져갈 듯 희미한 소리였다. 남자는 놀라 허겁지겁 아이에게 달려갔다.

—노마야!

이때, 뭔가에 발이 걸려 남자는 앞으로 고꾸라지고 말았다. 동시에 야구방망이에 맞은 것처럼 이마에 강렬한 통증을 느꼈다. 뭔가 와장창 부서지는 소리도 들렸다.

and didn't exist anymore as far as the city's building registry was concerned. Even with the danger of it collapsing at any time, blankets couldn't be happier to be able to live in the building at all, since its ceiling protected them from the rain. It had not been uncommon for an abandoned apartment or office-hotel building to cave in and kill hundreds of blankets at once. Yet no blanket was scared of being crushed to death under a falling building.

As the companies had relocated to the south of the river a long time ago, all the abandoned buildings on the northern side of the city had been occupied by blankets. Most of these people had moved in illegally, but even the police had never bothered chasing them out. Now that part of the city was a vast slum, where no one wanted to enter, except for gangs of youngsters from the Young Men's Association prowling the streets like packs of hyenas in search of prey.

As soon as he stepped inside in the darkness, the man's nostrils were assailed by the smell of liquor. At the same time, he heard his child moaning faintly, as if it was about to fade away. Startled, the man rushed toward the child.

"Noma!"

Just then, he tripped over something. As he fell

바닥을 나뒹굴며 신음하던 남자는 겨우 정신을 차리고 벽을 더듬어 스위치를 켰다.

　씨발!

　스위치를 올리자 깜박이는 백열등 아래 전모가 드러났다. 그가 걸려넘어진 건 토끼의 다리 때문이었다. 그녀는 팬티 하나만 걸친 채 술에 취해 잠들었는데, 기이할 정도로 새하얀 알비노의 알몸이 지저분한 잡동사니들 틈에서 녹아가는 눈사람처럼 널브러져 있었다. 그가 이마로 들이받은 테이블은 부서진 채 사방에 흩어져 있었다. 찢어진 이마에선 뜨끈한 피가 흘러내렸지만 그는 아픈 줄도 모르고 창가 소파에 누워 있는 아이에게로 엉금엉금 기어갔다. 아이는 죽은 사람처럼 얼굴이 창백했다.

　―노마야! 아빠야, 아빠!

　남자는 아이의 귀에 대고 이름을 불렀지만 아무 반응도 없이 작은 입에선 신음만 흘러나왔다. 그는 토끼에게 돌아가 다급하게 어깨를 잡아 흔들었다.

　―이봐, 정신 차려!

　그가 어깨를 흔들 때마다 축 늘어진 젖가슴이 힘없이 흔들렸다. 남자는 막장에 다다른 알코올중독자에게 아

over, he felt a terrible impact in his forehead, as if he had been hit by a baseball bat, followed by an intense pain. He also heard something shattering. After writhing and groaning on the floor for a while, he at last managed to find a light switch on the wall.

"Fuck it!"

The flickering lamplight revealed the situation. What had tripped him was Aunt Rabbit's legs. She was asleep and drunk, wearing nothing but under-pants. Her strangely white naked body lay sprawled on the floor in the middle of a mess of odds and ends, like a melting snowman. The table he had bumped his head against was smashed, its pieces scattered all over the floor. Warm blood flowed down from the gash in his forehead, but he no longer felt any pain while crawling toward his child, who was lying on a sofa by the window. The boy looked deathly pale.

"Noma! It's Daddy, Daddy's here!"

He leaned over the child's ear and called him, but there was no response except for a weak moan escaping its small lips. He returned to the woman and shook her by the shoulders urgently.

"Hey, wake up!"

Whenever he shook her, her droopy breasts

이를 맡긴 게 후회되는 한편, 아이를 버려둔 채 술에 취해 곯아떨어진 토끼에게 울화가 치밀었다.

—미친년!

화가 나 욕을 퍼부어도 아무 소용이 없었다. 그는 다시 소파로 달려가 아이를 둘러업었다. 하지만 막 문을 나서려는 순간, 그는 자신이 아무 데도 갈 수가 없다는 것을 깨달았다. 근처에 병원이 있긴 했지만 보험도 없는 담요를 들여보내줄 리가 만무했다. 당장 코앞에서 피를 흘리며 죽어가도 보험증서가 없으면 치료를 받을 수 없었다. 오래전, 그의 여동생도 그렇게 병원 앞에서 죽어갔다. 남자는 아이를 다시 소파에 누인 뒤, 무너지듯 바닥에 풀썩 주저앉았다. 그리고 토끼가 먹다 남은 술병을 집어들어 벌컥벌컥, 들이켰다. 담요들이 마시는 싸구려 중국산 밀주였다. 독한 술이 식도를 타고 넘어가자 가슴이 타는 듯했다.

토끼가 꿈틀, 몸을 움직였다. 그리고 게슴츠레 눈을 떠 옆에 주저앉아 흐느껴 울고 있는 남자를 바라보았다.

—왜 그래? 무슨 일이야?

그녀는 부스스 몸을 일으키며 물었다. 남자는 화를 낼 기분도 아니었다. 그래서 말없이 소파 위에 누워 있는

swayed limply. The man regretted having left his son in the care of this hopeless alcoholic. At the same time, he felt infuriated at Rabbit, who had drunk herself insensible, completely neglecting the child.

"You crazy bitch!"

But lashing out at her didn't help at all. So he hurried back to the sofa and lifted the boy onto his back. When he was about to walk out the door, though, he realized that he had no place to go. There was a hospital nearby, but he knew that they would never let him and his son in, two blankets with no health insurance. Even if a person was bleeding to death at the entrance of a hospital, he wouldn't be able to get any medical care without a certificate of health insurance. His younger sister had, long before, died like that in front of a hospital. After putting his son back onto the sofa, he flopped down on the floor. He then picked up the bottle lying beside Rabbit and gulped down the remaining liquor. It was cheap bootleg from China, the kind consumed by blankets. When the strong liquor went down his gullet, he felt a burning sensation in his chest.

Rabbit began stirring. Then she gazed, with bleary eyes, at the man sobbing beside her.

아이를 손가락으로 가리켰다. 그제야 토끼는 자리에서 일어나 아이에게 다가가 코에 귀를 대보았다. 그리고 상황을 파악한 듯 한숨을 내쉬더니 쓰레기 더미처럼 쌓여 있는 잡동사니를 뒤져 꼬깃꼬깃 접은 쪽지 한 장을 찾아냈다. 남자가 받아든 쪽지에는 몇 개의 숫자가 적혀 있었다.

—야매의사 전화번호야. 옛날에 회사원을 치료하다 의료사고를 내고 병원에서 쫓겨났는데 지금은 담요들 피를 빨아먹고 살지. 그래도 실력이 좋아서 회사원들도 가끔 찾는다니까 한번 연락해봐.

남자는 쪽지를 들고 놀란 눈으로 토끼를 올려다보았다.

—그리고 프리아는……

토끼는 맨가슴을 가릴 생각도 않은 채 남자가 들고 있는 술병을 가져가 한 모금 마신 뒤, 손으로 입가를 훔치며 말했다.

—죽었어.

*

병원은 버려진 건물 구석에 있어 겉으로 보기엔 병원

"What is it? What's the matter?" she lethargically raised herself and asked. The man didn't feel like getting angry with her anymore. So he silently pointed at the child lying on the sofa. Only then did Rabbit stand up and walk up to the child and put her ear to its nose. Uttering a sigh, as if she had finally gotten a clear grasp of the situation, she rummaged through the odds and ends on the floor that looked like a heap of trash, and pulled out a piece of crumpled-up paper. The man took it from her and saw some numbers written on it.

"A black-market doctor's phone number. He was kicked out of a hospital a long time ago for malpractice while treating an office worker. Now he makes a living by sucking up blood out of the blanket. But they say he's quite an able doctor and office workers still visit him now and then. Anyway, why don't you try giving him a call?"

The man looked up at Rabbit in surprise, holding the paper in his hand.

"And Friya—"

Rabbit didn't even bother covering her naked breasts when she took the bottle from his hand. After taking a swig, she wiped her mouth with the back of her hand and said, "She's dead."

인지 뭔지 알 수 없었다. 다만 한때 산부인과 병동이었던 듯 깨진 아크릴 간판에 ob/gyn란 글씨가 선명했다.

프리야가 죽었다고?

남자는 진료실 문 앞을 서성이고 있었다. 도대체 왜! 심장이 터질 듯 먹먹했지만 울음은 나오지 않았다. 행복을 찾아 벵골 만을 건넜던 가엾은 여자는 세상의 끝, 머나먼 반도에서 비참한 죽음을 맞았다. 자기 잘못이 아니어도 늘 미안하다고만 하던 착한 여자였는데 어쩌다가 악랄한 나치스트들의 먹잇감이 된 걸까? 그녀는 청년단 소속의 사내들에게 집단강간을 당한 뒤 잔인하게 살해되어 차가운 강물에 버려졌다고 했다. 도대체 왜! 단지 피부색이 다르다는 이유 때문에? 마침내 남자는 의자에 털썩 주저앉아 손바닥에 얼굴을 묻었다.

이때, 문득 의자 밑에서 뭔가 반짝이는 작은 물체가 눈에 들어왔다. 집어 들어보니 그것은 다름아닌 회사 배지였다. 의사가 실력이 좋아 회사원도 가끔 찾는다는 토끼의 말이 떠올랐다. 어떤 회사원이 병원을 찾았다가 바닥에 떨어뜨린 게 틀림없었다.

―보호자 들어오세요.

간호사가 안에서 남자를 부르자, 그는 재빨리 배지를

The clinic was located in a corner of an abandoned building; it was hard to know whether it was a really clinic from its outside appearance. The only clue was the acrylic sign with "ob/gyn" still clearly visible on it, which suggested that that corner of the building might once have been the obstetrics and gynecology ward of a hospital.

Friya's dead? the man was pacing up and down outside the examination room. Why on earth! he had a tight feeling in his heart, as if it was about to explode, but he couldn't cry. The poor woman, who had crossed the Bay of Bengal in search of happiness, ended up dying miserably in a faraway peninsula at the end of the continent. His wife had been a tenderhearted woman, ready to apologize, even when she was not at fault. 'How on earth has she fallen victim to the atrocious Nazis. He heard that she had been gang-raped and cruelly killed, and thrown into the cold river by some members of the Young Men's Association. Why on earth! Was it simply the color of her skin? In the end, the man collapsed on a chair, burying his face in his hands.

At the moment, something shiny under the chair caught his eyes. He picked it up and realized it was

주머니에 집어넣고 진료실로 들어섰다.

문제는 스테로이드 때문이었다. 의사는 아이의 작고 약한 몸에 무작정 스테로이드를 투여해 당뇨가 심해졌다고 했다. 그는 약물에 중독된 듯 쉴새없이 몸을 긁어대며, 당장 급한 대로 처치를 했지만 이대로 방치하면 아이가 얼마 못 살 거라는 말을 앵무새처럼 되풀이했다. 그리고 당장 병원에 가지 않으면 위험한 상태라고 했다. 여기가 병원인데 도대체 어디를 가란 말이지?

아이를 업고 집으로 돌아오는 길은 꽉꽉하기 그지없었다. 아이는 그의 등에서 잠이 들었다. 어떤 처치를 했는지 몸도 따뜻했고 숨소리도 일정했다. 보기와는 달리 토끼 말대로 진짜 실력이 있는 의사인지도 몰랐다. 하지만 그것은 어디까지나 임시방편일 뿐, 아이의 몸 안에서 어떤 끔찍한 일이 진행되고 있는지 알 수 없었다.

결국, 아이는 죽게 되는 걸까? 프리야처럼? 그리고 오래전 병원 앞에서 죽어간 그의 여동생처럼? 세상은 언제부터 이렇게 가혹해진 걸까? 그리고 왜 사랑하는 사람들은 늘 이런 식으로 곁을 떠나는 걸까? 인간은 원래 처음부터 그런 운명이었을까? 혹독한 시련과 고통, 불평등과 부조리, 착취와 굴종만이 삶의 조건인 것일까?

a company badge. He remembered what Rabbit had told him: the doctor was so competent that even office workers came to see him often. Some office worker must have visited the clinic and accidentally dropped his badge there.

"Where's the boy's guardian? Please, come in."

When the nurse called him from the inside, he quickly put the badge in his pocket and entered the examination room.

Steroids proved to be the culprit, not the cure. The doctor told him that the boy's diabetes had gotten worse because of the steroids recklessly dosed into his tiny, weakened body. Constantly scratching himself like a drug addict, the doctor repeated like a parrot that he had done what he could, but it was just a temporary measure and the boy would die soon if he was left untreated. The doctor added that the boy needed to be taken to a hospital right away.

I thought we came to a hospital. Where else could I take my boy? the man asked himself.

Heavy-hearted, he came back home, carrying his son on his back. The boy fell asleep on the way. He didn't know what exactly the doctor had done for his son, but now the child's temperature felt normal and his breathing regular. Unlike his ap-

어린 시절, 세상에 대한 느낌은 늘 따뜻했다. 비록 늘 지쳐 있지만 어딘가 믿음직스러운 아버지와 다정한 엄마, 자신이 누군가와 단단히 결속되어 있고 어딘가에 속해 있다는 뿌듯한 안심…… 그것은 마치 새 둥지처럼 아늑하고 부드러운 느낌이었다. 그런데 왜 그런 느낌은 다 사라지고 없는 걸까? 왜 모든 게 가혹하고 싸늘해진 걸까? 그것은 과연 누구의 잘못일까? 남자는 해답을 알 수 없는 질문과 혼돈에 사로잡힌 채 터덜터덜, 슬럼가 한복판을 걸어갔다.

*

식당 안에는 은은한 오보에 선율이 흐르고 있었다. 남자는 양복을 입고 식탁 앞에 앉아 메뉴판을 들여다보았다. 메뉴는 모두 영어로 적혀 있었다. 영어가 공용어가 된 이후, 한글은 담요들이나 쓰는 소수어가 되었다. 창밖에 보이는 거리의 간판도, 주변에서 식사하는 손님들의 대화도 모두 영어였다. 남자는 발레리노처럼 우아하게 테이블 사이를 오가는 웨이터들을 힐끗거리며 재빨리 메뉴판을 훑어보았다. 아는 단어가 몇 개 있긴 했지

pearance, the doctor could truly be an able one, as Rabbit had told him, he thought. But it was just a stopgap remedy, as the doctor had told him, and there was no way of knowing what terrible things were happening inside the child's body.

Is my boy going to die after all? Like Friya? Like my younger sister who died in front of a hospital long ago? When did the world become so cruel? And why do the people I love always leave me this way? Are all humans destined to live and die like this? Bitter trials and pain, inequality and absurdity, exploitation and servility—are these the only conditions of life? When he was a child, the world seemed to be warm and kind. With his reliable father, though he was always exhausted, and his affectionate mother beside him, he felt safe knowing that he was tightly bound up with others and belonged somewhere. It was a sense of being protected by something soft and cozy, like in a bird's nest. Why then has that feeling disappeared altogether? Why has everything turned cruel and cold? Whose fault is it anyway? Gripped in unanswerable questions and confusion, the man trudged across the central part of the slum.

만 어떤 종류의 음식인지 짐작이 가지 않았다. 아이도 낯선 분위기에 주눅이 든 듯 말없이 아빠의 눈치를 살폈다. 하지만 남자는 어깨를 펴고 보란 듯이 가슴을 앞으로 쭉 내밀었다. 그의 양복 왼쪽 가슴엔 금색의 회사 배지가 반짝거렸다.

야매의사를 만나고 온 다음날, 남자는 담당 조정관에게 전화를 걸었다. 그가 아이를 입양시킬 의향이 있다고 하자 그는 뜻밖의 수확에 만족해 껄껄 웃으며 잘 생각했다고, 축하한다고 했다. 아이를 입양 보내는데 축하라니! 어이가 없었지만 그는 입양절차에 관해 간단한 설명을 듣고 전화를 끊었다. 그리고 단 한 벌밖에 없는 양복을 꺼내 입었다. 아이에게도 제일 좋은 옷을 입혔다. 두 사람의 마지막 만찬을 위해서였다.

남자는 이런저런 막일을 하기 위해 회사원들이 일하는 구역에 몇 번 들어와본 적이 있었지만 그들만 다니는 전용식당에 들어온 건 처음이었다. 식당은 과연 짐작대로 호화롭고 우아한 분위기였다. 의자는 평생 앉아 있어도 좋을 만큼 편안했고 테이블 위엔 눈처럼 하얀 식탁보가 덮여 있었다. 그리고 실내엔 식욕을 자극하는 좋은 냄새가 퍼져 있었다.

＊

Soft oboe music was playing inside the restaurant. The man, wearing a suit, was reading the menu at a table. The menu was written in English. After English had become the official language, Korean had been reduced to a minority language used only by the blankets. All the signs along the street outside the window were in English; so were the conversations among the other diners near his table. The man, stealing glances at the waiters, walking elegantly, like ballet dancers around the tables, quickly skimmed the menu. He recognized a few words, but couldn't guess what kinds of food they were. The boy also seemed nervous, studying his father's face silently. Nevertheless, the man squared his shoulders and threw out his chest, as if to show it to the boy. On the left chest of his jacket shone a golden company badge.

The day after he had taken his son to the black-market doctor, the man had called the coordinator. When he said he was considering adopting out his boy, the coordinator had burst into laughter, excited with his unexpected windfall, and said that the man had made the right decision, and congratulated him. How on earth can this man congratulate

회사원을 사칭하는 건 매우 엄중한 범죄였다. 게다가 그는 음식값을 지불할 능력도 없었다. 식당에서 바우처를 받을 리도 없지만 남은 바우처마저 이미 아이의 치료비로 다 써버려 그야말로 무일푼 신세였다. 하지만 그는 아이와 제대로 된 식사만 할 수 있다면 아무것도 겁날 게 없었다. 어떤 일이 벌어진다 해도 지금의 상황보다 더 비참할 것 같진 않았다. 그래서 그저 될 대로 되라는 심정으로 당당하게 웨이터에게 음식을 주문했다.

—아빠, 우리 여기 매일 오면 안 돼?

아이는 남은 생선 부스러기와 크림소스를 포크로 싹싹 긁어먹으며 천진하게 물었다. 남자는 어이없다는 듯 웃었지만 그 또한 닦을 필요도 없을 만큼 깨끗하게 접시를 비운 후였다. 음식은 과연 눈물이 날 만큼 훌륭했다. 독특하고 날카로운 풍미가 오랫동안 입안에 감돌아 자꾸만 입맛을 다시게 만들었다. 그런데 왠지 이상한 슬픔에 가슴이 먹먹했다. 난생처음 맛본 훌륭한 음식에 감동해서인지, 아니면 그 좋은 것들로부터 평생 격리당한 억울함 때문인지, 그것도 아니면 아이와 영영 헤어져야 하는 슬픔 때문인지는 알 수 없었다. 다만 눈시울이 뜨거워져 자꾸만 천장을 올려다보았다. 아름다운 크

me on giving up my son for adoption? he was dumb-stricken, but just listened quietly to the co-ordinator's brief explanation of the adoption procedure. After hanging up, he had put on the only suit he had. He also helped his son get into his best clothes. It was to be their last supper together.

The man had, a few times, entered the work zones of the company employees in order to do some bit of odd labor, but this was the first time he had stepped in a restaurant frequented exclusively by them. As he had guessed, it indeed had a posh and elegant atmosphere. The chair he sat on was so comfortable that he thought he could spend his whole life on it; all the tables were covered with snow-white tablecloths, and the entire dining room smelled of wonderful foods, peaking the diners' appetites.

Impersonating a company worker was a serious crime. What's worse, he didn't have any money to pay for the meal. He was literally penniless after having spent all his saved-up vouchers on his boy's treatment at the clinic. Not that the restaurant would have ever taken vouchers anyway. Still, nothing scared him anymore—as long as he and his son could have a proper meal together. No matter what might happen later, it wouldn't be any more

리스털 샹들리에 불빛이 그의 얼굴 위에 쏟아져내렸다.

멀리서 웨이터가 계산서를 들고 다가오는 게 보였다.

그래, 가당치도 않은 호사는 여기가 끝이구나, 오히려 홀가분한 기분이었다. 그는 새삼 옷깃을 여미고 미구에 닥쳐올 사태를 담담하게 기다리고 있었다. 가능하면 조용히, 그리고 신속하게 일이 처리되었으면 좋겠다는 생각뿐이었다. 그런데 뜻밖의 상황이 벌어졌다. 웨이터는 그에게 다가와 음식값이 이미 지불되었다는 사실을 알려주었다. 그리고 구석 자리에 앉아 있는 한 노신사를 가리켰다. 등이 구부정하고 머리가 허옇게 센 노인은 식사를 다 마친 듯 등을 돌린 채 혼자 차를 마시고 있었다. 남자는 생면부지의 노인이 왜 대신 음식값을 냈는지 이유를 알 수 없어 어리둥절했다. 뭔가 착오가 생긴 걸까? 남자가 조심스럽게 노인에게 다가가자 그는 차를 마시다 문득 고개를 들었다. 그리고 서로 눈이 마주쳤을 때 남자는 놀라 눈을 크게 떴다.

—아버지?

삼십 년도 더 지났지만, 그래서 허리가 구부정해지고 주름이 깊어졌지만 남자는 자신의 아버지를 한눈에 알아보았다. 노인은 희미하게 웃으며 고개를 끄덕였다.

miserable than the state they were already in, he thought. So he confidently placed an order, telling himself: Whatever will come will come.

"Daddy, can't we come here every day?" the child asked innocently, while forking up the bits of fish and cream sauce remaining on his dish and eating them. The man gave him a bitter smile, but his dish was also scraped clean. The food was exquisite, to the point of bringing tears to his eyes. Its unique and keen flavors lingered in his mouth, making him smacking his lips repeatedly. Nonetheless, for some reason, there was a sense of unfamiliar sadness in his heart. Was he so deeply impressed by the wonderful food he had tasted for the first time in his life? Or was it because of this unfairness of being deprived of all these good things throughout his life? Or was it the sorrow from having to be separated from his child for the rest of his life? Not knowing which one was correct, he felt hot tears welling up in his eyes, and he kept looking at the ceiling. The light from a beautiful crystal chandelier poured down on his face.

Some tables away, he saw a waiter coming toward him with a bill.

Well, this unreasonable luxury is finally coming to an end, he felt rather relieved. He straightened

그리고 앉으라는 듯 눈으로 맞은편의 의자를 가리켰다. 남자가 엉거주춤 자리에 앉자 노인은 부드러운 목소리로 물었다.

　―그래, 맛있게 먹었니?

　맛있고 자시고 생각할 계제가 아니었다. 지난 세월의 온갖 복잡한 감정들이 한꺼번에 밀려와 입안에 쓴 침이 고였다.

　―도, 도대체 이, 이게 어떻게……!

　남자는 감당할 수 없는 혼란에 말을 더듬었다. 그러자 노인은 손짓으로 웨이터를 불러 물을 한 잔 가져다달라고 했다. 잠시 후, 남자는 웨이터가 가져다준 물을 벌컥벌컥 들이켰다. 그리고 한동안 숨을 몰아쉬다 문득 궁금증이 생겼다. 자신이 아버지를 알아본 것도 신통한 일이지만 아버지는 어떻게 자신을 알아본 걸까? 아버지가 집을 나간 건 그가 열 살 무렵의 일이었다. 용케 당시의 모습을 기억하고 있다 하더라도 중년이 된 자신을 알아본다는 건 불가능한 일이었다. 그런데 곧 의문이 풀렸다. 노인은 뒤쪽 테이블에 앉아 있는 아이를 가리켰다.

　―저 애 말이야. 너 어릴 때랑 꼭 닮았구나.

himself and waited calmly for the approaching crisis. His only wish was that it would be dealt with as quietly and swiftly as possible. But then something unexpected occurred. The waiter came up to him and informed him that his bill had been taken care of, and he pointed at an elderly gentleman sitting at a corner table, not far from them. The older man with a stooped back and white hair was drinking tea, perhaps having finished his meal, with his back turned to them. The boy's father was taken aback, not knowing why the old man, a total stranger to him, had paid for their meals. Has there been a mistake? he wondered. As he walked up to the table, the old man suddenly lifted his face from his tea cup. When the two looked into each other, the younger man's eyes widened in surprise.

"Father?"

More than 30 years had passed, so his father's back was bent and his wrinkles deepened. Nevertheless, the man recognized him right away. The old man gave a faint smile and nodded at him, and signaled him with his eyes to sit down opposite him. As the man sat down, awkwardly, the old man asked him in a soft tone, "Well, have you enjoyed the meal?"

It was no occasion for them to discuss whether the food had been good or bad, thought the man.

아이는 후식으로 나온 아이스크림을 떠먹으며 남자가 있는 테이블 쪽을 힐끗거리고 있었다.

─그런데 눈이 크고 얼굴이 검은 걸 보니까 에미가 이쪽 사람이 아닌 모양이지?

늘 전쟁을 치르듯 혹독하기만 한 자신의 삶과 대비해 아버지의 모습이 너무나 평온해 보여 남자는 눈앞에 펼쳐지는 장면이 꿈속인 듯 도무지 현실감이 없었다.

─근데 왜 에미는 안 데리고 온 거니?

순간, 남자는 울컥 화가 치밀었다. 그래서 자신도 모르게 볼멘소리로 말을 내뱉었다.

─프리야는 죽었어요.

─프리야? 그럼 인디아에서 온 여자로구나. 그런데 어쩌다가⋯⋯?

여전히 평온한 목소리였다. 그러게 조심하지 않고 어쩌다가 넘어졌니, 하는 듯한 말투였다. 거기엔 조직에 오랫동안 몸담았던 회사원 특유의 절제와 무기력이 엿보였다. 남자는 질문에 대답도 않고 수십 년간 마음속에 품어왔던 의문을 아버지 앞에 꺼내놓았다.

─근데 왜 우리를 버리신 거예요?

남자의 떨리는 말투엔 분노와 회한, 원망과 서러움이

So many complicated emotions from the past rushed into his mind, and he felt bitter saliva collecting in his mouth.

"What—what on—what on earth—!" the man stuttered out of a confusion beyond his control.

The old man called the waiter with a gesture and asked him to bring a glass of water. Shortly, the man gulped down the water. While he was breathing hard, to collect himself, it dawned on him that there was something curious about their meeting. It was miraculous enough that he had been able to recognize his father after all these years. But how on earth had his father recognized him? He had been ten when his father had walked out on the family. His father may have been able to remember his childhood face, but it was impossible for him to recognize his now middle-aged son. Soon the puzzle was unraveled, though, when the old man pointed at the boy sitting at the table behind him.

"That boy there, he looks exactly like you when you were a child."

His son was stealing glances at him and the old man while eating the dessert: ice cream.

"But his eyes are bigger and his skin's darker. His mother is not Korean, is she?"

In contrast to the man, who had lived such a

응어리져 있었다.

—내가 너희를 버렸다고? 누가 그런 소릴 하디?

—엄마가요. 다른 여자가 생겨서 우릴 버리고 떠난 거라고요.

남자가 따지듯 묻자 아버지는 발끈해서 핏대를 세웠다.

—그 망할 놈의 여편네가 그런 소릴 해?

순간, 엄마와 부부싸움을 하던 아버지의 옛 모습이 되살아났다. 하지만 그는 곧 다시 차분하고 힘없는 노인으로 돌아갔다.

—애야, 그건 오해란다. 다른 사람은 몰라도 넌 이해해야 해.

그는 뭔가 난처한 듯 주변을 살피며 냅킨으로 이마의 땀을 닦았다.

—그럼 왜 한 번도 찾아오지 않았어요? 미숙이가 죽은 건 알고 계세요? 병원비가 없어서 치료도 한 번 못받고 죽어갔는데 왜 한 번도 연락이 없었던 거예요, 왜!

남자는 자신도 모르게 버럭, 소리를 질렀다. 식사하던 손님들이 일제히 남자 쪽을 쳐다보았다. 그때 그는 문득 식당 안의 손님들이 모두 아버지 또래의 노인들이라는 사실을 깨달았다. 다들 양복을 입고 있었는데 한결

harsh life, as if he was constantly at war with the world, his father seemed so peaceful that the man felt what was happening before his eyes was unreal, like a dream.

"Why haven't you brought your wife with you?" his father asked him.

At the moment, anger surged up in the man. He spat out, in spite of himself: "Friya's dead."

"Friya? Then, she was from India, wasn't she? But what on earth happened—?"

The old man maintained his peaceful tone—a tone one might use saying things like "Well, you should have been more careful not to fall down." It smacked of the temperance and languor of an office worker, someone who had been working for the same system for a long time. Without bothering to answer the question, the man brought up what had been harboring in his heart for decades.

"Why on earth did you abandon us?"

In the man's trembling voice were anger, regret, resentment, and sadness all at once.

"I abandoned you? Who told you that nonsense?"

"Mother told me that you had left us for another woman."

At the man's adamant demand for an explanation, the old man turned purple with anger.

같이 머리가 허옇게 세고 허리가 구부정해 마치 고급
요양시설에 와 있는 느낌이었다. 그러고 보니 아버지가
입고 있는 회색 양복도 어딘가 눈에 익었다. 옆에 놓여
있는 가죽가방도 그가 어릴 때 본 바로 그 서류가방이
었다. 도대체 어떻게 된 거지, 남자는 갈수록 머릿속이
혼란스러워 컵에 남은 물을 마저 들이켰다.

─미안하다. 미숙이에 대해선 입이 열 개라도 할 말이
없지만 내가 여자 때문에 집을 나갔다는 건 정말 오해
란다.

아버지는 잠시 분위기가 가라앉을 때를 기다려 다시
입을 열었다.

─도대체 뭐가 오해라는 거예요?

─난 사실 집을 나간 적이 한 번도 없어.

아버지의 목소리엔 어딘가 안타까움이 서려 있었다.

─그게 무슨 소리예요? 아버진 삼십 년 동안 한 번도
집에 들어오신 적이 없잖아요.

남자가 계속 몰아붙이자 아버지는 마침내 더 이상 참
을 수 없다는 듯 버럭 소리를 질렀다.

─난 집을 나간 게 아니라……!

그의 노기 서린 목소리엔 짙은 슬픔이 배어 있었다.

"That cursed woman told you that?"

His father's fury suddenly reminded him of the old quarrels between his father and mother. In the next moment, however, the old man was back to his usual, calm and weak self.

"Dear son, that's a misunderstanding. I don't know about other people, but you, my son, must understand that's not what's really happened."

The old man seemed nervous about something, looking about him and wiping the sweat off his forehead.

"Why then haven't you come home at all? Do you know Mi-suk's dead? She'd never had a chance to be treated at a hospital before she died, because we didn't have money to pay for it. All these years, you've never contacted us, not even once. I want to know why!"

The man yelled at the old man unwittingly. All the other diners turned their eyes to him. Only then did he notice that most of the diners in the restaurant were people his father's age. All of them were dressed formally and had gray hair and a stooped back. It was as if he was in a high-class home for seniors. Come to think of it, his father's gray suit somehow looked familiar too. Even the leather briefcase lying beside him was the same one he

어느새 눈시울도 붉어졌고 주름 잡힌 눈꺼풀이 파르르 떨렸다. 그는 울음을 참기 위해 앙다문 이 사이로 남은 말을 힘겹게 뱉어냈다.

　─아직 퇴근을 못 하고 있는 거야.

had seen as a child. 'What's going on?' Getting more and more confused, the man drank up the water in the glass.

After waiting for their intense emotions to cool down, his father opened his mouth again, "I'm sorry. I've got no excuse whatsoever when it comes to Mi-suk's death. But it's not true that I've left my family for another woman."

"Which part of it have I misunderstood?"

"To tell the truth, I've never left home."

A sense of frustration could be detected in the old man's voice.

"What d'you mean? You've never returned home for 30 years."

Driven to the wall by the man's repeated accusations, the old man burst out yelling as if he couldn't stand it anymore, "It's not true that I haven't come home!"

His angry voice gave away a sense of profound sadness. Tears stood in his eyes and his wrinkled eyelids trembled. He clenched his teeth to fight back his tears and struggled to finally utter:

"I couldn't have left the office because I haven't finished my work yet."

Translated by Jeon Miseli

창작노트
Writer's Note

「퇴근」을 쓰겠다고 결정한 것은 불과 마감 1주일 전이었다. 하지만 소설에 대한 구상은 매우 오래 전에 시작되었고 그것은 순전히 MB 덕분이었다. 왜냐하면 그가 권력을 손에 넣었을 때부터 나는 한국의 미래에 대해 많은 근심과 우려를 갖지 않을 수 없었기 때문이었다.

「퇴근」은 한국의 미래사회를 배경으로 하고 있다. 미래란 과거에서 현재로 이어지는 선을 연장한 것이다. 따라서 나는 과거에서 현재로 이어진 선이 어디로 향하고 있는지를 알면 미래를 짐작할 수 있다고 믿는다. 이에 대해 나는 가능한 한 합리적이고 과학적인 관점을

It was only a week before the deadline when I decided to write "Homecoming." However, the story had been taking shape in my mind for a long time. And I owe it entirely to Myung-bak Lee (the 17th president of Korea, 2008-2013), because I could not help being greatly concerned and fearful for the future of Korea when he came to power.

"Homecoming" has a future Korean society as its setting. The future is always part of a continuum extending from the past through the present. Therefore, I believe, if we know the direction taken by historical developments, we will be able to conjecture a future. While writing "Homecoming," I made an effort to maintain as rational and scientific

유지하려고 애썼다. 하지만 후에 다시 작품을 읽어보니 어쩔 수 없이 그 안에는 나의 절망과 분노가 담겨 있다는 것을 깨달았다.

산업화 이후, 모든 이들의 꿈은 회사원이 되는 거였다. 회사원이 되는 것이야말로 양질의 삶을 보장받을 수 있는 유일한 길이라는(불안한, 그래서 더욱 신실해야만 하는) 믿음이 있었기 때문이었다. 회사원이 되기 위해선 대학에 가야 했고 그래서 다들 기꺼이 끔찍한 학창시절을 견뎌냈다. 하지만 그 달콤한 꿈은 이제 악몽이 되어 실업의 공포와 비정규직의 절망만이 어두운 그림자를 드리우고 있다. 과연 희망은 있을까?

인간은 누구에게나 상대를 지배하고 조종하고 착취하려는 욕망이 있다. 그것은 자유에 대한 갈망과 지배에서 벗어나려는 의지보다 언제나 더 강력하다. 그래서 역사는 힘을 가진 극소수의 사적 욕망에 의해 지배되고 결정되기 마련이다.

이제 곧 전 세계 상위 1퍼센트가 소유한 자산이 나머지 99퍼센트의 자산보다 많아질 거라고 한다. 또한 하

a viewpoint as possible. Nevertheless, when I read the work again, some time later, I realized that it is inevitably imbued with my despair and indignation.

With the industrialization of the country, working for a company as a salaried employee became everyone's dream. People believed—with some uneasiness, and therefore more fervently—that it was the only guaranteed path to a good life. To become a salaried office worker, they had to go to the university and endure horrible campus life. That sweet dream, however, has turned into a nightmare; and now the dread of unemployment and despair of temporary workers cast dark shadows over Korean society. Is there any room for hope?

All humans have a baser desire to dominate, manipulate, and exploit others. This desire is always stronger than their craving for freedom or their will to escape domination. Thus, history is doomed to be controlled and determined by the personal desires of a very few powerful people.

It is said that the top one percent of the world will soon possess more wealth than the remaining 99 percent. Further, the assets of the bottom 50 percent are less than one percent of the world's

위 50퍼센트가 소유한 자산은 전체 자산의 1퍼센트에도 미치지 못한다. 이런 불평등에 대해 대부분은 어쩔 수 없는 문제라고 생각한다. 누군가 문제를 제기하면 그는 곧 위험한 인물로 낙인이 찍힌다. 조지 오웰이 예견한 전체주의의 모습이 현실이 되고 있다. 한국의 경우, 친일자산가를 중심으로 군부독재시절에 형성된 군벌과 이제는 슈퍼리치가 된 기업가들, 그리고 그들과 결탁한 관료들의 힘이 너무나 막강해졌다. 식민지 시대부터 한 세기 동안 그들은 그야말로 눈부신 성공을 거두었다. 그리고 돈과 조직, 언론과 정보를 독점한 그들에게 대항할 상대는 이제 아무도 없게 되었다. 의심할 바 없는 완전한 승리에 박수를! 짝짝짝!

「퇴근」은 아직 벌어지지 않은 미래에 대한 이야기를 담고 있다. 하지만 거기엔 지금 현재, 우리의 현실을 이해할 수 있는 단서가 담겨 있다. 그것이 진짜 현실이 될지, 아니면 그저 소설적 상상으로 끝날지는 알 수 없으나 비록 허구라 하더라도 소설은 현실을 파악하고 들여다보는 강력한 도구라는 믿음에는 여전히 변함이 없다.

total. Most people think that this inequality is inevitable. If someone else takes issue with their opinion, he or she gets branded immediately as a dangerous person. The totalitarianism foreseen by George Orwell is now becoming a reality. In Korea, the military clique formed during the period of military dictatorship, with the pro-Japanese men of property in the center and the entrepreneurs-turned-super-rich and bureaucrats allied with them have become too powerful. Over a century since the colonization of Korea by Japan, they have achieved literally dazzling success. And now there is no one who can confront these groups, who monopolize money, organizations, the press, and information. Give them a big hand for their undeniable, sweeping victory! Clap-clap-clap!

"Homecoming" is a story about a reality that has not arrived yet. Nevertheless, it contains clues that can help us to comprehend our present situation. I do not know whether this future will come true or simply continue to be my novelistic imagination. Even if it remains a made-up story, though, I still firmly believe that fiction is a mighty tool with which we can look into and get a clear grasp of reality.

해설
Commentary

'21세기 자본'에 새겨진 조감도

정은경 (문학평론가)

마르크스는 자본주의 파멸을 예기하면서 '갈수록 소수의 손에 집중되는 자본'을 그 근거로 들었고, 『21세기 자본』의 토마 피케티는 역사적–경험적 자료를 통해 이 불평등을 입증한 바 있다. 마르크스의 종말론은 축적된 자본으로 인해 자본 수익률이 줄면, 자본가들 사이에 격렬한 투쟁이 일어나거나 혹은 국민소득 가운데 자본가의 몫이 무한히 증가하여 노동자들이 폭동을 일으켜 자본주의를 끝장낼 수 있다는 것이다.

마르크스의 프롤레타리아 대동단결과 해방은 이제 한물 간 이데올로기가 되었지만, 토마 피케티에 의해 확인된 '부의 편중'은 그 실증적 자료와 함께 더욱 실감

"Homecoming": A View of Extreme Inequality

Jung Eun-kyoung (literary critic)

Karl Marx based his argument for the downfall of capitalism on "capital being accumulated in the hands of an ever decreasing number of capitalists." Thomas Piketty, in his *Capital in the Twenty-First Century* (2013), demonstrates this inequality using historical and empirical data. According to Marx's eschatology, when the rate of capital profit accumulation decreases due to the greater accumulation of capital, either violent struggles take place among capitalists themselves or their share of the national income keeps increasing, leading to labor riots and eventually the demise of the capitalist system.

Although Marx's idea of the grand union and lib-

을 얻어가고 있다. 양극화의 심화, 실업률의 증가, 암암리에 성행하고 있는 음서제, 신분 상승 사다리의 격감, 중산층의 파괴 등등. 우리 사회는 피케티가 『21세기 자본』에서 진단한 바로 그 사회로 급강하하고 있음을 부인할 수 없다. 즉, 자본의 힘이 점점 더 강해지고 자본의 소득 몫이 커지며, 자본이 자본을 낳는 이른바 세습자본주의(patrimonial capital)의 사회 말이다.

천명관의 「퇴근」은 마르크스와 토마 피케티가 가리키고 있는 자본주의의 종말 혹은 이후를 그린 디스토피아적 미래가상소설이다. 천명관이 아마도 현실의 지표를 따라가 당도했을 법한 '이후'의 세계에서는 10%의 슈퍼리치들이 모든 것을 소유하고 세상을 굴리며 90%의 실업자를 먹여 살린다. '담요'라 불리는 90%의 실업자들은 '일'과 거기에 부수된 일상과 존엄 등등에서 제외된 채 정부에서 나눠주는 바우처를 받아 최소한의 생계만을 유지하고 있다. 이들 세계에서 구성원들의 꿈은 '회사원이 되는 것'이고 10%의 회사원들은 이들과 분리된 저쪽의 고층빌딩에서 '컴퓨터'를 통해 자본을 증식시킨다.

이러한 곳에서의 슈퍼리치 이외의 삶이란, 굳이 상상

eration of the proletariat has become an outdated ideology, Piketty's "disproportionate concentration of wealth" and the empirical data he uses has proven true to increasing numbers of observers. Today's intensification of socio-economic polarization, increasing unemployment rates, high-handed personnel administrations operating in the dark, sharp decreases in opportunities to rise on the social ladder, a breakdown of the middle class—all of these conditions manifest the undeniable symptoms of contemporary society rapidly turning into the one prognosticated in *Capital in the Twenty-First Century*—that is, the present world is changing into the so-called patrimonial capitalistic society, where capital begets capital, as its power grows and the capitalists' share of the income increases.

Cheon Myeong-kwan's "Homecoming" is a dystopia, a story of an imagined future depicting the endgame of capitalism and its aftermath, as has been prophesied by others, including Marx and Piketty. Guided by the trends in our current reality, Cheon's imagination reaches a probable society of post-capitalism. In that society, the richest 10 percent of the population, the "super-rich," possess everything, manipulate the world, and feed the unemployed, i.e., the remaining 90 percent. The un-

하지 않아도 될 만큼 현재 세계 곳곳에 볼 수 있는 극빈자들, 실업자들, 난민들의 그것과 닮아 있다. 첫 장면은 고용공단 사무실에서 길게 줄을 서 있는 수천 명의 '실업자'들의 풍경에서부터 시작한다. 이들 사이를 가로지르는 '조정관'들과 '삐끼'들이 뒤엉켜 만든 풍광에는 "핵 공격을 받은 중동에 투입될 용병을 모집하거나 제약회사의 피실험자들, 장기판매 안내"가 적힌 찌라시들이 나부끼고, 조정관들은 언제까지 이 무용지물들을 먹여 살리느니 '살처분'하는 것이 낫겠다고 투덜거린다.

이 줄에 끼어 있는 주인공인 '그'에게 '바우처'는 더욱 더 절실한 것인데, 그것은 천식을 앓고 있는 아이의 약을 구해야 하기 때문이다. 남편의 학대를 피해 한국에 건너온 인도 여성과 가죽 공장에서 만나 결혼했으나 공장이 문을 닫자 여자는 이들을 떠났다. 홀로 아이를 돌봐야 하는 '그'는 거의 굶다시피 해서 아껴둔 바우처로 암시장에서 스테로이드를 구입해 아이를 치료한다. 하여 그에게 삶은 그야말로 서바이벌일 수밖에 없는데, 그런 그에게 고용공단 조정관은 솔깃한 제의를 한다. 아이를 슈퍼리치에게 입양을 하라는 것이다. 몇 년 전부터 슈퍼리치들 사이에선 아이를 입양하는 게 유행이

employed, called "blankets," pick up a scanty liveli-
hood on the vouchers issued by the government,
having been deprived of any chance to "work," i.e.,
to perform a daily routine, and thereby to feel dig-
nity. In the world of "Homecoming," becoming a
salaried office worker is everybody's dream; and
the office workers, that is, the super-rich, work in
the high rises on one side of the city, separated
from the blankets, and busy proliferating their capital using computers.

One does not need to stretch the imagination in
order to envision the life of the 90 percent in this
story, since it is not very different from the condi-
tion of the destitute, unemployed, and displaced all
over our world.

"Homecoming" opens with a scene inside the office of the Employment Corporation, which is
packed with thousands of people out of work
standing in long queues. In the same office are the
"coordinators," who would rather have all the
homeless "killed off" than feed the "useless free-
loaders" forever; and the "touts" who thread their
way in and out of the queues, handing out flyers
"for recruiting mercenaries to be dispatched to the
Middle East " or "inviting participants into experiments conducted by pharmaceutical companies,"

었는데, 자신의 부와 노블레스 오블리주를 과시하기 위한 것이다. 입양 제의를 한 귀로 흘렸던 '그'였지만, 알코올 중독자이자 이웃집 여성인 '토끼 아줌마'에게 맡긴 아이가 혼절하자 생각을 바꾼다. "아이의 작고 약한 몸에 무작정 스테로이드를 투여해 당뇨가 심해졌으며, 당장에 병원에 가지 않으면 위험한 상태"라는 야매의사의 말 때문이다.

그는 아이를 데리고 회사원만이 출입할 수 있는 레스토랑에 가서 마지막 만찬을 즐긴다. 무일푼인 그가 어떤 곤욕을 치러야 하는 지점에 이르자, 옆 테이블의 한 노신사가 그들의 음식 값을 내준다. 알고 보니 그 노인은 그가 열 살 때 집을 나갔던 것으로 알았던 아버지였던 것이다. '그'가 여동생의 불행한 죽음과 버림받은 자신의 처지를 들먹이며 아버지를 비난하자, 노인은 그에게 소리를 지른다. 집을 나간 게 아니고 "아직 퇴근을 못 하고 있는 거야."

'퇴근하지 못한 아버지'와의 극적인 상봉이라는 결말이 극심한 빈부 격차, 실업자 아버지와 천식을 앓는 아이 등의 흥미진진한 문제제기를 잘 봉합하는 방식이라고 볼 수 없으나 이 작품이 애초에 제기한 '문제의식'은

or "trafficking in human organs."

The protagonist, referred to as simply "the man" or "he," is standing in one of the lines. His voucher is essential because he has to get medicine for his child who is suffering from asthma. After the initial scene, the story turns back to the time when the man, then working in a hide tanning factory, falls in love and lives with an Indian woman, who has come to Korea to escape her abusive husband. Once the factory closes, however, his wife leaves him and their child. Raising his sick child by himself, he must starve himself to save for the vouchers to buy steroids for asthma on the black market. For him, life is an endless struggle to survive. Then one of the coordinators at the office makes him a tempting offer: that he adopt out his child to a super-rich. For a few years, it has been a fad among the super-rich to adopt children as a way of showing off their wealth and spirit of noblesse oblige. At first, the man does not give the suggestion much thought, but when his child faints while in the care of Aunt Rabbit, an alcoholic neighbor, he changes his mind. A black-market doctor tells him, "the boy's diabetes had gotten worse because of the steroid recklessly dosed into his tiny, weakened body," and that the boy will die if he is not

이러한 다소 황당한 '끝맺음'을 넘어설 만큼 흥미롭고 강력하다. 그것은 「퇴근」의 세계가 사실 먼 미래가 아니라 '현재적' 실감 위에 있기 때문이다. 고액을 벌기 위해 제약회사의 피실험자가 되는 생동성 아르바이트, 장기 밀매, 파병 지원 등등은 말할 것도 없고, 과시와 부자의 관용의 경계를 오가는 입양 문제, 갖은 스펙과 기술을 갖춘 고급 인력 양성과 상관없는 증가하는 청년 실업률, 그리고 '1:99'로 기억되는 월스트리트의 시위에 이르기까지 「퇴근」은 좀 더 높은 곳에서 내려다 본 현재의 '조감도'라 할 수 있다.

마르크스, 토마 피케티와 더불어 2050년쯤이면 전통적인 산업 부문을 관리하고 운영하는데 전체 성인 인구의 5%만 필요할 것이라는 제레미 리프킨의 『노동의 종말』까지 덧붙인다면 「퇴근」의 90% 실업률은 가상이 아니라 무시무시한 진짜 현실이 될 수 있다. 그저 일상에 널린 기계들, 하이패스, 세콤, 현금 인출기 등은 점점 '인간의 노동'을 소멸 혹은 해방시키고 있는 것들이 아닌가. 그러니 토마 피케티가 『21세기 자본』에서 강조한 중요한 결론, "부의 분배와 역사는 언제나 매우 정치적인 것이었으며, 순전히 경제적인 메커니즘으로 환원될

taken to a hospital right away, which makes the man resolved to give up his child for adoption.

He takes his child to a restaurant reserved for office workers and they enjoy their last supper together. When the impoverished father is about to suffer the bitter insult of not being able to pay the bill, an elderly gentleman sitting nearby pays for their meal. Coincidentally, the old gentleman turns out to be the man's father, who walked out on his family when the protagonist was ten years old. When the man blames his father for the miserable death of his younger sister and his own hard life, his father yells at him that it is not true that he left his family, adding: "I haven't been able to come home because I haven't finished my work yet."

The protagonist's dramatic encounter with this long-lost "father who has not been able to leave his office" may not be the most effective way to resolve the issues raised in the story, such as the vast gap between haves and have-nots, a younger father who cannot find work, and his child suffering from asthma. Nevertheless, the writer's awareness of the problems, notable throughout the story, is intriguing, and intense enough for the reader to look beyond this rather absurd ending.

The world of "Homecoming" represents not

수 없다. 불평등의 역사는 관련되는 모든 행위자가 함께 만든 합작품이다"라고 했던 그 '인간 주체'는 불평등의 역사에 대한 통찰과 함께 다시 회복되어야 한다.

정은경 문학평론가. 1969년 서울에서 태어나고 고려대 독문과와 국문과 대학원을 졸업했다. 2003년 《세계일보》에 평론 「웃음과 망각의 수사학」으로 등단하였으며, 현재 아시아 문학전문 바이링궐 계간지 《아시아》의 편집위원으로 활동하고 있다. 2005년 고려대학교에서 「한국 근대소설에 나타난 악의 표상」으로 문학박사학위를 취득했으며, 현재 원광대 교수로 재직 중이다. 저서로 『디아스포라 문학』 『한국 근대소설에 나타난 惡의 표상 연구』 『지도의 암실』 등이 있다.

some remote future, but a clear sense of present reality. Consider all the aspects of our present world: part-time work as test subjects in biological experiments conducted by pharmaceutical companies in exchange for money, illicit organ trafficking, the recruitment of soldiers for foreign wars, adoption by the rich that blurs the line between showing off and noblesse oblige, increasing youth unemployment rates, regardless of a variety of skills and specialties, and the Occupy Wall Street protest with its division of society into the 1 percent and 99 percent. As such, "Homecoming" can be called a trenchant view of our present reality.

In addition to Karl Marx and Thomas Piketty, if we take into consideration Jeremy Rifkin's prediction in *The End of Work* that by 2050, it will take only 5 percent of the world's adult population to manage and operate all the traditional industries, the 90 percent unemployment rate in "Homecoming" may not be a fantasy, but rather a probable and macabre reality of humanity in the future. Is it not the case that most of the machines we use today for our daily necessities, such as ATMs and other electronic devices, are eliminating the need for human labor?

In the conclusion of *Capital in the Twenty-First Cen-*

tury, Piketty contends: "The distribution and the history of wealth have always been very politically oriented, and thus cannot be restored to purely economic mechanisms. The history of inequality is the work of collaboration among all involved and all related agents." The notion of "human agency" here must be recovered, along with keen insight into the history of inequality.

Jung Eun-kyoung Born in Seoul in 1969, Jung Eun-kyoung graduated from Korea university after majoring in German and Korean literature. She made her literary debut by winning *the Segye Ilbo* Spring Literary Competition in criticism with the article "A Rhetoric of Laughter and Forgetting: on Song Sok-ze." Her published works include *Literature of Diaspora, A Study of the Representation of Evil in Modern Korean Novels*, and *A Darkroom of Map*. She is currently a professor at the Division of Korean Language and Literature at Wonkwang University and a member of the editorial board of the magazine of Asian literature *ASIA*.

비평의 목소리
Critical Acclaim

천명관은 한국문학의 영토에 슬며시 잠입해 들어온 낯선 이방인과도 같다.

이정석, 「실재에 대한 강박에서 벗어난 서사」,

《문학동네》, 문학동네, 2007

결론적으로 말해 이 작가는 전통적 소설 학습이나 동시대의 소설작품에 빚진 게 별로 없는 듯하다. (……) 이 작가에게 이 대목이 이 소설에 왜 필요하냐고 묻는 것은 무의미하다. 이야기로서의 위력이면 그만이기 때문이다. 심지어 자신이 황당한 이야기를 했다 싶으면 스스로, 세상에 그런 일이 어디 있겠어요? 그렇지요? 라고 익살을 부린다. 자신만의 독특한 스타일을 만들어냈다는 점에 동의하지 않을 수 없다.

은희경, 「제10회 문학동네소설상 심사평」,

《문학동네》, 문학동네, 2004

Cheon Myeong-kwan is like a stranger who has infiltrated the territory of Korean literature.

Yi Jeong-seok, "A Narrative Away From the Obsession for Reality," *Munhakdongne*, 2007.

In conclusion, this author does not seem to owe much to traditional creative writing training or contemporary narratives... It is meaningless to ask why this particular sentence is necessary in that particular short story. All that matters to him is the power of storytelling. After writing something outrageous, he even acts funny and asks: "Would that have really happened? What do you think?" I cannot help agreeing to some people's comments that he has created his own unique style.

Eun Hee-kyung, "A Judge's Remark for the 10th Munhak dongne Novel Award," *Munhakdongne*, 2004.

K-픽션 008
퇴근

2015년 4월 17일 초판 1쇄 발행
2019년 4월 10일 초판 3쇄 발행

지은이 천명관 | 옮긴이 전미세리 | 펴낸이 김재범
기획위원 정은경, 전성태, 이경재
편집 김형욱, 강민영 | 관리 강초민, 홍희표 | 디자인 나루기획
인쇄·제책 굿에그커뮤니케이션 | 종이 한솔PNS
펴낸곳 (주)아시아 | 출판등록 2006년 1월 27일 제406-2006-000004호
주소 경기도 파주시 회동길 445(서울 사무소: 서울특별시 동작구 서달로 161-1 3층)
전화 02.821.5055 | 팩스 02.821.5057 | 홈페이지 www.bookasia.org
ISBN 979-11-5662-115-7(set) | 979-11-5662-118-8 (04810)
값은 뒤표지에 있습니다.

K-Fiction 008
Homecoming

Written by Cheon Myeong-kwan I Translated by Jeon Miseli
Published by ASIA Publishers I 445, Hoedong-gil, Paju-si, Gyeonggi-do, Korea
(Seoul Office: 3F, 161-1, Seodal-ro, Dongjak-gu, Seoul, Korea)
Homepage Address www.bookasia.org I Tel. (822).821.5055 I Fax. (822).821.5057
First published in Korea by ASIA Publishers 2015
ISBN 979-11-5662-115-7(set) | 979-11-5662-118-8 (04810)

한국의 잃어버린 얼굴 Traditional Korea's Lost Faces

해방 전후(前後) Before and After Liberation

전후(戰後) Korea After the Korean War

K-픽션 한국 젊은 소설

최근에 발표된 단편소설 중 가장 우수하고 흥미로운 작품을 엄선하여 출간하는 〈K-픽션〉은 한국문학의 생생한 현장을 국내외 독자들과 실시간으로 공유하고자 기획되었습니다. 원작의 재미와 품격을 최대한 살린 〈K-픽션〉 시리즈는 매 계절마다 새로운 작품을 선보입니다.